WHY WE BECAME RESCUE HEROES™

The Teammates Tell Their Exciting Stories

by J. E. Bright

SCHOLASTIC INC.

New York   Toronto   London   Auckland   Sydney
Mexico City   New Delhi   Hong Kong   Buenos Aires

ISBN 0-439-41909-3

Fisher-Price, Rescue Heroes, Billy Blazes, Smokey, Ariel Flyer, Jake Justice, Wendy Waters, Gil Gripper, Nemo, Matt Medic, Kenny Ride, Rocky Canyon, Claude, Sandy Beach, Willy Stop, Roger Houston, Comet, Warren Waters, Sergeant Siren, Al Pine, Wind Chill, Sam Sparks, Jack Hammer, Bill Barker, Buster, Hal E. Copter, Rip Rockefeller, Bob Buoy and related trademarks, copyrights, and character designs are used under license from Fisher-Price, Inc., a subsidiary of Mattel, Inc., East Aurora, NY 14052 U.S.A. ©2002 Mattel, Inc. All Rights Reserved.

Manufactured for and distributed by Scholastic Inc.
Published by Scholastic Inc.
SCHOLASTIC and associated logos are trademarks and/or registered trademarks of Scholastic Inc.

12 11 10 9 8 7 6 5 4 3 2 1   2 3 4 5 6 7/0
Printed in the U.S.A.
First printing, December 2002

Years ago, the Rescue Heroes were children, too. They played with their friends and went to school. But then there was one special moment in each of their lives when something changed.

Seeing real rescues was incredibly important to those children. It showed them that bravery and training can make a big difference. And it inspired them, so when they grew up, they became...

RESCUE HEROES!

Billy Blazes

FIREFIGHTER

When I was little, I took the battery out of my bedroom smoke alarm to use in a video game. There was a fire in our hallway a month later. I woke up with smoke coming from under the door. I yelled for help.

"Stand back!" shouted a voice. Then a giant ax smashed the door open. A strong firefighter carried me out to safety.

That firefighter was awesome with his ax — and I wanted to be just like him!

After that, I always keep a good battery in my smoke alarm!

Now I am a firefighter, too, with my daring Dalmatian, Smokey, by my side. He rushes into burning buildings to help victims, and carries a water cannon to put out fires.

Ariel Flyer

PILOT AND VETERINARIAN

When I was little, I went to a horse ranch. We were allowed to watch a mare giving birth.

But something went wrong. The mare and her baby were in trouble.

The ranchers couldn't handle the problem alone. They called a veterinarian who lived miles away. The vet showed up in a little plane. She was able to save the mare — and her baby.

When I saw the newborn foal stand up on his wobbly legs, I knew I would become a veterinarian . . . and a pilot!

That's just what happened, too! I get help from my pet hawk, who acts like my eye in the sky. He alerts me to dangers he spots from above.

Jake Justice

MOTORCYCLE POLICE OFFICER

When I was eight, I saw a couple of kids sitting in back of a truck behind my parents' car on the highway. I gasped when one of the truck's tires suddenly blew out. The truck swerved. The kids in the back couldn't hold on.

One boy was tossed over the side. He barely managed to hold onto the edge of the truck bed.

A highway patrol officer on a motorcycle zoomed up behind the screeching pickup. The officer grabbed the boy and pulled him to safety.

I knew then I wanted to be a motorcycle police officer, too.

Wendy Waters

FIREFIGHTER

I grew up with a hero in my own house — my father, Warren Waters. He was so amazing that I never thought he needed help to do anything. Then one night the house next door caught fire.

My father called 911. He rushed over there. But the old woman who lived inside was too sick for him to move by himself. So he kept her safe until the fire squad arrived and rescued both of them.

Seeing how bravely my father and the other fire fighters acted was a big inspiration for me. And I learned that rescuing takes teamwork!

Gil Gripper

SCUBA DIVER

It was the most frightening day of my childhood.

My grandmother parked her car on a wooden pier. I had already run down to the beach when the pier collapsed. The car slid into the water — with my grandmother still in it!

I was terrified...until a scuba diver swam down to the sunken car. The diver helped my grandmother escape. He shared his oxygen with her as he brought her up.

I will never forget that scuba diver's courage.

Every day I rescue people the same way. Luckily, a brave dolphin named Nemo helps me. Victims can hold onto his life buoy and be pulled to safety!

™

Matt Medic

Our quarterback broke his leg on my junior high football field. It was during a big game. I ran over to him and yelled for help.

A doctor ran down from the stands. He had me keep our quarterback calm. The doctor set my teammate's leg and loaded him onto a stretcher. Then our quarterback was quickly taken to the hospital. He had to wear a cast for awhile, but he was fine after that.

The doctor's quick action saved my friend from any extra pain. I knew then I wanted to help injured people the same way.

Kenny Ride

BICYCLE PATROL

When I was seven, my mother took me to an amusement park for my birthday. She had saved up for months to afford the trip.

Less than ten minutes after we arrived, some guy snatched my mother's purse. We quickly lost sight of the running man in the crowd of people.

We both started shouting for help. Immediately, a patrolman on a bicycle zoomed through the crowd. He caught the thief and returned my mother's purse.

That patrolman saved our vacation. And I realized that fighting crime can make people very happy!

Rocky Canyon

MOUNTAIN RANGER

It was a beautiful day when three of my friends and I began our hike up the mountain.

When we were halfway up a sheer cliff, the sky got dark. A sudden downpour soaked us. We huddled on a ledge, trapped! It was getting very windy. . . .

That was when a mountain ranger buzzed down in a helicopter. He lowered down a rope. One by one, he rescued us from that ledge.

He was amazing — risking his own life to save ours. Being a ranger seemed like the most exciting and rewarding job in the world.

It still seems that way! Now I patrol the wilderness with a mountain lion named Claude. He carries a backpack with a rescue hook and a compass so he's ready for any emergency!

LIFEGUARD

I spent a lot
of time on the beach
as a little boy. But I didn't
understand how powerful the
ocean truly is until my uncle came to visit.

He was jumping in the waves when he got pulled far
out in a sudden riptide!

I screamed for help. Quickly a lifeguard dove into the
ocean and pulled my uncle to shore.

How cool was that? Cool enough for me to want to be
a lifeguard from that moment on!

Willy Stop

On the street in front of my elementary school, a giant gasoline truck toppled over and began leaking fuel all over the road.

With a single spark, it could have blown up the entire school!

I will always be grateful to the police officer who arrived on the scene. He calmly led all the children and teachers to safety.

That showed me how important it is to keep order when something goes wrong. Now I stay calm during a crisis — no matter what!

Roger Houston

ASTRONAUT

As a boy, I visited one of the first weather stations in space. It sure wasn't as hi-tech as the Space Station is now!

During my visit, the commander of the weather station spotted a giant hurricane forming off the African coast — before anybody on Earth knew about it!

Because of that early warning, not one person was injured by the hurricane.

That taught me the importance of learning about disasters before they happen. And now I've dedicated my life to doing exactly that — from space!

I'm not alone up here — a monkey keeps me company! Comet loves to be silly, but I know I can count on him. He sends out signal satellites from his space vehicle to find lost explorers.

Warren Waters

When I was a rookie in the fire department, my squad was called in to help three other squads with a big fire in a museum.

The firefighters were lost in the smoky museum hallways, getting in one another's way.

My squad commander took charge. Calmly, he gave orders, helping us work together.

From my commander I learned how to lead rescue workers. I have never forgotten the importance of working as a team.

Sergeant Siren

POLICE OFFICER

I grew up near a tall mountain range. It had been raining nonstop for a few days, and there was a danger of flash floods.

My mother was driving me to a store down in a valley when we heard a loud voice on a megaphone. It was a police officer, telling us to head for the high ground. The flood was coming!

We got out of the valley just before the flood rushed through it.

I knew I wanted to spend the rest of my life warning people about disasters — before they struck!

ARCTIC HERO

In junior high school, I went on a snowboarding trip. My best friend and I were awesome snowboarders, so we left everybody else behind.

While we were on a difficult trail, my friend hit a tree . . . and broke his leg.

That's when we heard a terrifying rumbling from high up on the mountain. An avalanche! We yelled for help.

Before the avalanche burst through the forest, a ski patrolman whizzed up to us on a snowmobile. He got us out of there — fast!

Now I patrol icy mountains myself. And I love every minute of it!

I especially love working with Wind Chill, a friendly Saint Bernard. He rescues stranded mountain climbers and skiers with a backpack that converts to a stretcher or a sled.

Sam Sparks

FIREFIGHTER

When I was little, I was woken up by flashing lights and sirens outside my window — which was on the tenth floor of an apartment building!

The apartment across the street was on fire. My best friend lived over there!

Then the fire department arrived — with a ladder truck. They quickly raised their hoses and doused the flames, saving everyone inside.

I swore when I grew up I would learn to fight fires in hard-to-reach places, just like those heroes did that night. And that's just what I've done!

Jack Hammer

CONSTRUCTION EXPERT

The town I grew up in was built near a dam in a river. One day we heard a horrible creaking. A crack was creeping up the concrete face of the dam!

Everybody panicked. So many people tried to drive out of town that everybody got stuck in traffic.

Then a helicopter arrived at the base of the dam, and a rescue construction specialist got out. He repaired the crack — and it was even stronger than before.

After seeing what that construction worker could do, I wanted to be just like him.

Bill Barker

CANINE POLICE

My family always went to the woods for summer vacation. One year, my little sister wandered off — and got lost in the forest!

We searched for her all night, but the sun rose and we still hadn't found a trace of her.

The police brought in a dog team. We gave a dog my sister's shirt to smell. He ran into the woods, barking and sniffing the ground.

The dog tracked down my sister. She was caught in an old drainpipe. We quickly freed her. She was scared, but she wasn't hurt at all.

I gave that dog a big hug, and he licked my face... and suddenly I knew the best way to spend my life.

Now I work with Buster — the best police dog in the business! With his highly sensitive nose and piercing siren, Buster tracks down missing people and sounds the alarm. He also explores tight spots where humans can't fit.

Hal E. Copter

FLYING FIREFIGHTER

I was camping with my Boy Scout troop when all these panicked animals started running past us!

Our troop leader immediately knew what was going on. A forest fire! We packed up and ran for the road.

But we were cut off by the roaring flames.

A squadron of helicopter firefighters zoomed down and scooped us up. We got to ride in the copters while gallons of water were dropped onto the fire, dousing it.

It was the most exciting night of my life.

Rip Rockefeller

CONSTRUCTION WORKER

I grew up in tornado country.

The biggest twister hit my town when I was eleven. My family took shelter in our storm cellar. It was terrifying to hear our house being destroyed above us!

After the tornado passed, we couldn't open the cellar doors. We were trapped under the rubble!

It took a whole day for the rescue workers to clear the area enough to free us.

We all hugged the workers who opened the doors. One of them was the man who built our storm cellar! Its sturdy construction protected us from harm.

That's when I realized that building a strong shelter can save lives — before disaster strikes!

Bob Buoy

COAST GUARD

One day at the beach, my little sister fell asleep on her raft — and floated out to sea!

She was crying and hollering from the raft, but we could barely hear her.

Then the Coast Guard zoomed over to her in their speedboat and pulled her aboard, safe and sound.

The look on my mother's face when she hugged my sister made me want to join the Coast Guard that minute. But I had to wait until I was old enough!

Rescue Heroes!

Each Rescue Hero has a reason to save lives, but one thing is true for them all . . . they make the world a safer place to live in!

Copy that!

Safety Tips

REMEMBER TO THINK LIKE A RESCUE HERO — THINK SAFE!

 Dial 911 in an emergency

 Memorize your address and phone number in case you are ever lost

 Never play with matches

 Swim with a buddy — and only when there's a lifeguard on duty

 Make sure a grown-up knows where you are at all times

 If you're ever in a smoky building, stay close to the floor where the air is clearest

 When it's cold, dress in layers

 When it's hot, drink lots of water